DEPRESSION

How to Heal My Broken Heart from Rejection?

DANIEL CLARK

<u>DEDICATION</u>

This book is dedicated to all those who have experienced the pain of rejection and the darkness of depression. You are not alone.

To those who feel lost and broken, remember that it's okay to feel this way. It's okay to hurt, it's okay to not be okay. Your feelings are valid, and they matter.

To those who are in the midst of their healing journey, keep going. Healing is not linear, and it's okay to have bad days. Remember, every step you take, no matter how small, is progress.

And finally, to those who have healed and found their light, your strength is inspiring. Your story gives hope to others that they too, can overcome.

May this book serve as a hope, a guide to healing.

Remember, you are stronger than you think, braver than you believe, and loved more than you know.

It all started on a languid Sunday afternoon. The sun was at its zenith, casting long shadows that danced on the walls of my room. I found myself stirring from a restless slumber, my eyes reluctantly opening to the harsh light of noon. The previous night had been a long one, filled with a relentless parade of thoughts that kept sleep at bay.

She was the epicenter of my thoughts, her memory a haunting melody that played on an endless loop in my mind. Our shared moments, once a source of joy, had now become poignant reminders of what once was. Her laughter, her voice, the way her eyes lit up when she smiled - they were all etched in the deep recesses of my mind, refusing to fade away.

The echoes of our shared laughter reverberated in the silence of my room, a cruel reminder of the dreams that now lay shattered. Each memory was like a piece of a jigsaw puzzle, fitting together to form a picture of a time when happiness was a constant companion. But now, those pieces seemed to cut through my soul, leaving a trail of longing and despair.

Erasing her from my memory was an impossible task. Each attempt only served to bring her image into sharper focus, her absence a gaping void that seemed to consume everything in its path. Life, as I knew it, had become a grueling battle, each day a struggle to piece together the fragments of my broken self, each moment a fight to find meaning in the chaos. The world outside moved on, oblivious to my struggle, while I was trapped in a time warp, a prisoner of my memories.

As the days turned into weeks, and weeks into months, the pain of her absence became a constant companion. It was as if I was living in a parallel universe, one where she was a ghost, a specter that haunted every corner of my existence. The world outside continued its relentless march toward the future, but I was stuck in a past that refused to let go.

Her absence was like a black hole, consuming everything in its path, leaving behind a void that was impossible to fill. The laughter, the shared moments, the dreams - they were all sucked into this void, leaving behind a silence that was deafening. The echoes of our shared laughter, once a source of joy, now seemed like a cruel joke, a mockery of the happiness that once was.

The room, once filled with the warmth of her presence, now felt cold and empty. The walls, once adorned with our shared memories, now stood bare, stripped of the joy that once filled them. The silence was oppressive, a constant reminder of the emptiness that now defined my existence.

Each day was a battle, a struggle to find meaning in the chaos. The pain of her absence was a constant companion, a reminder of the love that once was, and the happiness that now seemed like a distant dream.

But despite the pain, despite the despair, I clung on to the memories, for they were all I had left of her. They were a reminder of a time when life was beautiful and when happiness was more than just a fleeting moment. They were a testament to a love that was, a love that could have been, and a love that would forever remain etched in the annals of my heart.

And so, I trudged on, carrying the weight of my broken heart, living each day in the shadow of her memory, hoping that one day, the pain would lessen, the void would fill, and life would find a way to move on. But until then, I was a prisoner of my memories, trapped in a past that refused to let go, living a life that was a mere shadow of what it once was.

Our first encounter was at a bustling coffee shop, a haven for coffee lovers nestled in the heart of the city. The place was alive with the hum of conversations, the clinking of cups, and the rhythmic hiss of the espresso machine. I was there with my friends, soaking in the lively atmosphere, the aroma of freshly brewed coffee wafting through the air like an invisible thread connecting all the patrons. We found a cozy corner and settled down, our laughter and chatter adding to the symphony of sounds around us, a harmonious blend of life's simple pleasures.

Across the room, she sat alone, engrossed in her thoughts, her fingers wrapped around a coffee mug like it was a precious relic. She was a vision of beauty, her tall frame draped in a simple dress, her curled hair cascading down her shoulders like a waterfall at twilight. Her African American heritage was evident in her striking features - the high cheekbones, the almond-shaped eyes, and the grace with which she carried herself. She was like a painting come to life, each detail more captivating than the last.

My eyes were drawn to her like a moth to a flame, and I found myself unable to look away. It was as if time had slowed down, the world around me fading into a blur. All I could see was her, her presence filling up the room, casting a spell that I was more than willing to succumb to.

Her solitude intrigued me. Amidst the hustle and bustle of the coffee shop, she seemed to be in a world of her own, her thoughts her only company. I wondered what she was thinking, what dreams danced in her eyes, what stories her silence whispered. I wanted to know her, to understand her, to be a part of her world.

As I sat there, lost in my thoughts, I realized that this was more than just a fleeting attraction. It was a connection, a pull that I couldn't resist. It was as if an invisible thread had tied us together, a thread that tugged at my heart each time I looked at her. I knew then that this was the beginning of a journey, a journey that would change my life forever. And so, with a heart full of hope and a mind full of dreams, I decided to take the first step, unaware of where it would lead me. Little did I know, this was just the beginning of our story.

As she finished her coffee and rose to leave, a sense of urgency gripped me. It was as if time had suddenly accelerated, each second ticking away with a ruthless efficiency. I couldn't let the woman who had unknowingly captured my heart, just walk away into the sea of faces, becoming another stranger in the crowd. I had to know more about her, to hear her voice, to know her name.

I followed her discreetly, careful not to draw attention to myself. My heart pounded in my chest as I navigated through the bustling streets, my eyes never leaving her figure. She moved with an effortless grace, her every step a dance in itself. The world around us seemed to blur into insignificance, the noise of the city fading into a distant hum. She walked down the bustling streets, her silhouette weaving through the crowd, a solitary figure in the sea of faces. The city, with its towering buildings and endless roads, seemed to bow to her grace, creating a path for her. She finally stopped in front of a building on 25 Street Park Avenue, her destination reached.

The sight of her walking away stayed with me, etched in my memory like a painting. The way her hair swayed with her movements, the way her dress clung to her figure, the way she disappeared into the building - it was a sight that would haunt my dreams for days to come.

As I stood there, on the bustling streets of the city, I realized that I had begun a journey. A journey that started in a coffee shop, with a woman whose name I didn't know, but whose memory had captivated my heart. I didn't know where this journey would lead me, or what the future held for me. But I knew one thing for sure - I was willing to take the risk, to follow my heart, to see where this path would lead me. For in the end, isn't that what life is all about? Taking risks, following your heart, and hoping for the best. And so, with a heart full of hope and a mind full of dreams, I took the first step towards an unknown future.

The next morning, I woke up with a sense of purpose that was as invigorating as the first rays of the sun. The events of the previous day had sparked a flame within me, a flame that was fueled by the desire to know more about her. With a newfound determination, I found myself back at the coffee shop, this time alone. The familiar aroma of coffee filled the air, but this time, it was accompanied by a sense of anticipation.

As I pushed open the door, the chime of the entrance bell echoed through the room, announcing my arrival. I scanned the room, my heart pounding in my chest. And then, our eyes met. She was there, sitting at the same spot, her presence filling the room like a melody fills the silence. It was as if everything had conspired to bring us together again.

I waved at her, a simple gesture that carried the weight of my intentions. She looked up, her eyes meeting mine, and responded with a gentle smile. It was a smile that held the promise of a thousand unsaid words, a smile that reached her eyes and warmed my heart. It was as if the sun had decided to rise in the middle of the coffee shop, casting a warm glow on everything around it.

There was an innocence about her that was incredibly endearing. It was reflected in her eyes, in her smile, in the way she sipped her coffee. It was as if she carried a piece of something special within her, a piece that was untainted by the harsh realities of the world. This innocence added to her allure, making her seem like a beacon of light in a world that was often too dark.

As I stood there, taking in the sight of her, I realized that this was more than just a chance encounter. It was a dance choreographed by destiny, a dance that had just begun. And I, entranced by her charm, was more than willing to follow the rhythm. Little did I know, this dance would lead me on a journey of self-discovery, a journey that would change the course of my life forever. And so, with a heart full of hope and a mind full of dreams, I took the first step towards an unknown future.

With a deep breath to steady my nerves, I made my way across the room towards her table. The short distance seemed like a marathon, each step echoing the pounding of my heart. I stood before her, a question hanging in the air between us. "May I join you?" I asked, my voice barely above a whisper. Her response came in a soft, childlike voice that was music to my ears, "Yes, you may."

I introduced myself as Jeremy, extending a hand towards her. She took it, her grip firm yet gentle, and shared her name - Alicia. That day, we conversed like old friends meeting after a long time, sharing stories from our past, our dreams for the future, and laughter that filled the room. Time seemed to lose its meaning, hours passing like fleeting moments, and before we knew it, the day had come to an end.

From that day forward, the coffee shop became more than just a coffee place. It became our meeting point, a place where our love story unfolded, one cup of coffee at a time. We were inseparable, each day spent in each other's company bringing us closer. The bond we shared was intense, a palpable connection that was felt more than it was seen. Our conversations over coffee turned into shared meals, long drives exploring the city, and seaside dinners under the starlit sky.

Our daily meetings at the coffee shop turned into a ritual, a part of our day that we both looked forward to. We explored the city together, each street, each corner revealing a new aspect of our relationship. The city, with its towering buildings and bustling streets, became a silent witness to our growing bond.

The seaside dinners were a world in themselves. Under the starlit sky, with the sound of waves as our music, we shared our deepest fears and highest hopes. The sea, with its endless expanse, seemed to mirror the depth of our feelings for each other.

As days turned into weeks, and weeks into months, our bond only grew stronger. We were two bodies but one soul, our hearts beating in a rhythm that was all our own. Our love story, which started in a bustling coffee shop, had now become a saga of shared dreams, endless conversations, and a bond that was as deep as the ocean. And through it all, the coffee shop remained our constant, a symbol of our journey, a testament to our love.

Our love story was like a beautifully written novel, each

chapter more captivating than the last. The coffee shop, our first meeting point held a special place in our hearts. It was as if destiny had chosen this quaint little place to unite our paths together. Each coffee date was a new page in our story, each conversation a new paragraph, and each shared laughter a new sentence. Our love story continued to unfold there, one coffee date at a time, the aroma of freshly brewed coffee a constant backdrop to our growing affection.

A year had passed since our first encounter, and our love had only deepened with time. Like a tree that grows stronger with each passing season, our bond had grown stronger with each passing day. I had decided to take the next step, to ask her to be my life partner, and to begin a lifelong journey together.

With a heart full of hope and a pocket full of dreams, I tried reaching out to her at her residence, but she wasn't there. Her absence felt like a void, a silence that was too loud. I dialed her number, each ring echoing the beating of my anxious heart. But my calls went unanswered, each unanswered call adding to the growing storm of anxiety within me.

Impatience started to gnaw at me like a relentless tide eroding a rock. Doubts and worries began to cloud my mind, casting long shadows over my hopeful heart. Questions raced through my mind - Where was she? Why wasn't she answering? Was she okay? The uncertainty was a bitter pill to swallow.

I waited for her call, each passing moment feeling like an eternity. But it never came. The silence of my phone was a harsh reminder of the distance that had suddenly sprung up between us. But amidst the storm of emotions, I held onto our shared memories, hoping that soon, the storm would pass, and the skies of our love story would be clear once again.

Driven by desperation and a sense of urgency, I found myself standing in front of her residence. The familiar path that I had walked so many times before now seemed alien. The door, once a symbol of warmth and welcome, stood cold and locked. She was gone, her absence echoing in the silence of the empty house.

I was left baffled and dumbfounded, like a sailor lost at sea. The world around me seemed to spin, my mind a whirlpool of questions and confusion. Where had she gone? Why had she left without a word? The silence of the house was a harsh reminder of the reality that had befallen me.

Days turned into nights, and nights into days, but my attempts to reach her were in vain. I kept trying her number, each unanswered call adding to the growing despair within me. The sound of the dial tone was a cruel reminder of the distance that had come between us. It was as if I was trying to reach out to a ghost, a shadow of the woman I had fallen in love with.

And then, one day, when hope was nothing more than a flicker, I finally managed to get through to her. The sound of her voice on the other end of the line was like a ray of light piercing through the darkness. It was a moment of relief, a moment of hope, a moment that promised the possibility of answers. But it was also a moment of fear, for I did not know what those answers would be. Would they bring relief, or would they bring more pain? Only time would tell.

The dam of patience had finally broken, and a torrent of frustration flooded out. I found myself shouting at her, each word a reflection of the anguish and despair that had been building up inside me. I told her how her sudden disappearance had driven me to the brink of insanity, how each passing day without her was like a dagger to my heart. I was upset, my emotions spilling over, tears streaming down

13

my face as I sobbed uncontrollably. The silence from her end was deafening, amplifying the sound of my beating heart.

And then, she finally spoke. Her voice was soft, almost a whisper, like the rustling of leaves in a gentle breeze. She said, "My husband called me. He needed me by his side." The words hit me like a bolt of lightning, leaving me stunned. Husband? She was married? The revelation was like a punch to the gut, leaving me winded.

She had never mentioned her husband. We had grown so close over the past year, and shared so many memories, so many moments of joy and laughter, but she had never uttered a word about being married. It felt like the ground beneath me had shifted, the world as I knew it, crumbling around me. The woman I had fallen in love with, the woman who had become an integral part of my life, was someone else's. The realization was a bitter pill to swallow. It felt like I was trapped in a nightmare, desperately hoping to wake up. But the harsh reality stared back at me, its gaze unwavering.

The silence that followed was heavy, filled with unsaid words and unshed tears. The love story that had blossomed over countless cups of coffee, under the starlit sky, had taken a turn I had never anticipated. It was a twist in the tale that left me grappling with a whirlpool of emotions - shock, disbelief, and a profound sense of loss. The path that lay ahead was uncertain, shrouded in the shadows of the shocking revelation. But one thing was clear - nothing would ever be the same again.

I found myself arguing with her, my voice a reflection of the disbelief and hurt that was coursing through me. "Why didn't you tell me?" I asked the question hanging in the air between us like an accusation. The silence that followed was deafening, the tension palpable.

Then, she confessed. Her husband had been having an affair with another woman. He had betrayed her trust and cheated on her, but despite it all, she still loved him deeply. It was a love that was rooted in years of shared memories and experiences, a love that refused to be erased by his betrayal. She had tried to forget him, to erase him from her heart and mind, but had failed. His memory was like a ghost, haunting her, refusing to let go. Then she met me, and for a while, life seemed perfect. Everything seemed right. Our shared moments, our laughter, our conversations - they were like a balm to her wounded heart.

But deep down, there was a tiny ray of hope within her, still yearning for his love and touch. It was a hope that was hidden in the deepest corners of her heart, a hope that was kept alive by the memories of their shared past. It was this hope that had held her back, that had kept her from fully embracing the love that we shared.

Her confession left me reeling, a whirlpool of emotions threatening to consume me.

Betrayal, hurt, disbelief - they all fought for dominance, leaving me feeling lost and confused. The woman I had fallen in love with, the woman who had become an integral part of my life, was tied to another man by the threads of love and betrayal. It was a revelation that shook the very foundation of our relationship, leaving me to pick up the pieces of my broken heart. Her confession left me shattered. Amidst the chaos, I knew I had to find a way to heal, to move on from this devastating revelation. It was going to be a long and painful journey, but I was ready to face it. After all, life goes on.

As she revealed the truth about her husband, my heart plummeted into an abyss of despair. It felt as if the ground beneath me had given way, and I was free-falling into a chasm of heartbreak. The woman I had loved, the woman who had been the center of my universe, was already bound to another man. My world, which had once been filled with dreams of our shared future, crumbled around me in an instant.

The plans I had meticulously crafted, of proposing to her, of us becoming husband and wife, of raising a family together, were shattered into a million pieces. The dreams that had once brought me joy were now a source of unbearable pain. I felt as if I was choking, gasping for breath in a reality that was too harsh to accept.

The misery, like a relentless winter storm, wrapped its cold, unforgiving arms around me. It threatened to drown me in a sea of sorrow, its icy waves crashing over me with ruthless intensity. I felt as though I was being pulled under, the weight of the truth anchoring me to the ocean floor.

Her words, which once flowed like a soothing balm, healing and comforting, now felt like shards of ice. They pierced my heart with their cold, hard reality, each word a dagger of betrayal. The warmth that her voice once held was replaced by a chilling aloofness, the transformation as stark as a summer day turning into a winter night.

Each syllable was hard to swallow, like a bitter pill. They echoed in the hollow chambers of my heart, their sound a cruel reminder of the bitter truth. The truth was that she was not mine, that she belonged to someone else. The truth is that our love story, which seemed so perfect, was marred by a reality that was as harsh as it was unexpected.

The world around me seemed to blur, the colors of joy and happiness fading into shades of grey. The laughter, the shared moments, the dreams - they all seemed like fragments of a beautiful dream, a dream from which I had been rudely awakened. The echo of her confession rang in my ears, a constant reminder of the love that could have been, but was not meant to be.

As I grappled with this new reality, I realized that love, as beautiful as it is, can also be a source of profound pain. It can build us, and it can break us. But despite the pain, despite the heartbreak, I knew that I would cherish the memories we made, the love we shared. For they were a testament to a love that was real, even if it was not meant to last. And in the end, isn't that what truly matters? To have loved and lost, then to have never loved at all.

Suddenly, there was silence. A deafening silence that echoed the turmoil within me. What could I possibly say to her? Could I have pleaded with her to stay? Would she have listened? Would she have chosen me over her husband?

These questions haunted me, their answers elusive. The silence between us spoke volumes, a poignant reminder of the love we had shared and the heartbreak that now lay between us. The woman of my dreams was now a painful memory, a reminder of a love that could have been but was never meant to be. The journey ahead was going to be a difficult one, filled with healing and acceptance. But one thing was certain - this experience had changed me, and I would never be the same again.

In the throes of despair, I found solace in the bitter embrace of alcohol. It was a desperate attempt to numb the pain that gnawed at my soul, a pain so profound that it made me contemplate the unthinkable - ending my own life. I tried, with every fiber of my being, to move on, to forget, to heal. But the memories of our time together were relentless, haunting me like specters in the night.

She was once mine, my pride, my joy. But now, she belonged to another man, a reality that was a dagger to my heart. The knowledge that I could never have her back was a bitter pill to swallow, a constant reminder of what I had lost.

As the days turned into weeks, and weeks into months, the world around me seemed to mirror my inner turmoil. The days grew darker, the nights colder, as if nature itself was mourning my loss. The warmth of her love, which once was my comfort, now tormented my sleep. I was caught in a vicious cycle of sleepless nights and tear-filled days.

I would lock myself in my room, surrendering to the overwhelming sadness that washed over me. My tears were the silent testament to my broken heart, the physical manifestation of my inner torment. What was once a life filled with happiness and laughter had turned into a bleak existence filled with sadness and despair.

The rejection was a hard blow. She was my world, my everything. But to her, it seemed, my feelings didn't matter. She had moved on, leaving me behind, lost and alone in the wilderness of my emotions. It was as if I was a mere footnote in her life, easily forgotten, easily replaced.

She never apologized and never showed any signs of remorse. It was as if I never existed in her life. This indifference was perhaps the most painful of all, a constant reminder of how insignificant I was to her. It was a harsh reality that I struggled to accept, a reality that threatened to consume me.

But despite the pain, despite the despair, I knew I had to keep going. For even in the darkest of nights, there is always the promise of a new dawn. And so, I trudged on, carrying the weight of my broken heart, in the hopes of finding light amidst the darkness.

My friends, those who had been close to me, began to notice the change. They reached out, their voices filled with concern as they rang me up, trying to understand my situation. They tried their best to console me, to bring back the person they once knew. But there was a void within me, a gaping hole that seemed impossible to fill. It was a pain that was hard to put into words, a rejection that was difficult to explain.

One day, in an attempt to clear my mind, I decided to step out of my self-imposed isolation. I went for a walk, hoping that the fresh air would somehow cleanse my soul, and provide some respite from the torment. As I walked, I noticed her. She was with her husband, a wealthy Irish businessman. He was her new world, her new love.

I looked at her, hoping, even if for a fleeting moment, that she would notice me. That she would acknowledge my presence, greet me with a smile, a nod, anything. But she simply ignored me, walking away without a second glance. It was as if I was a stranger, an insignificant part of her past that she had chosen to forget.

She seemed happy, genuinely happy. Her eyes sparkled with joy, her laughter echoed in the air, and her smiles were brighter than I had ever seen. She looked at him the way she used to look at me, her eyes filled with love and admiration. It was as if she was experiencing love at first sight, all over again.

Seeing her so happy, so in love, was a harsh reminder of what I had lost. It was a painful realization that she had moved on, that she had found happiness in the arms of another man. And all I could do was watch, my heart breaking a little more with each passing moment.

My mind was a whirlwind, a tempest of questions that refused to be silenced. Why did she behave that way toward me? Why did she choose to hide the truth? She knew she was married, she knew the implications of her actions. Yet, she chose to keep me in the dark, to let me believe in a future that was never meant to be.

Every moment we spent together, every laugh we shared, every secret we whispered, was now tainted with the harsh reality of her betrayal. She could have confessed, she could have been honest with me. But she chose silence, she chose deception.

The realization was like a punch to the gut, a cruel reminder of the deceit that had been woven into our relationship. It was a bitter pill to swallow, the knowledge that our love, our connection, was built on a foundation of lies.

I was left grappling with the aftermath, trying to make sense of the chaos that my life had become. The woman I loved, the woman I thought I knew, was a stranger. And I was left picking up the pieces of my shattered heart, trying to find a way to move forward.

But amidst the storm of questions, one thing was clear - I deserved better. I deserved honesty, I deserved respect, I deserved love. And with that realization, I found the strength to pick myself up, to face the world again. Because no matter how painful the truth may be, it is better than living a lie. And so, I chose to move forward, to heal, to grow. Because I knew, deep down, that this was not the end of my story, but merely the beginning of a new chapter.

With a heavy heart and a mind full of questions, I decided to confront her. The very next day, I stationed myself outside her building, my eyes scanning the entrance for any sign of her. The moment she stepped out, I followed her at a safe distance, my heart pounding in my chest. I had made up my mind to question her, to seek answers to the questions that had been tormenting me.

She entered a supermarket and I followed suit, maintaining a considerable distance so as not to alert her of my presence. She seemed oblivious to my presence, engrossed in her world. Seizing the opportunity when she was alone, I approached her. With a firm grip on her hand, I led her to a secluded corner of the supermarket.

"Alicia," I began, my voice trembling with a mix of anger and pain, "Why did you behave so indifferently towards me? We were in love, weren't we?"

She looked at me, her eyes welling up with tears as she replied, "Jeremy, I was very disturbed and upset when we met. I was at my weakest moment. I was feeling lonely and shattered."

Her words stoked the fire of anger within me. "Why did you

use me?" I retorted, my voice rising in fury. "Was I just a fling for you? A play toy? You were married all that time we were together and you never uttered a word."

"Yes, I was married," she admitted, her voice barely above a whisper. "I didn't want to mention it to you. My husband was having an affair with his friend's wife. All I needed was love desperately. I noticed you too were longing for the same but Jeremy, I'm tremendously sorry because you misunderstood me. I didn't have any feelings for you. It was just a sort of temporary feeling that existed for a short time between us. I love my husband immensely and now he's come back to me."

Her words were like a slap in the face. "I'm sorry but I don't want you anymore in my life. I want you to stop bothering me and stop contacting me. If you come anywhere closer to me I will have you arrested."

Her words echoed in my ears, each syllable a painful reminder of the harsh reality. I was left standing there, my heart shattered into a million pieces, as she walked away, leaving me alone once again in the wilderness of my emotions.

I stood there, rooted to the spot, as her words echoed in my ears. The woman I had loved with every fiber of my being, the woman I had given my heart to, was telling me that our love was nothing more than a fleeting distraction for her. A wave of emotions crashed over me - anger, betrayal, sadness. It was a maelstrom that threatened to consume me.

I wanted to scream, to let out the pain that was tearing me apart. I wanted to shout at her, to make her understand the depth of the hurt she had inflicted. I wanted to tell her how much she had broken me. But the words wouldn't come. All I could do was stand there, silent and broken, a shell of the man I once was.

With a heavy heart, I turned away from her, from the supermarket, from the life I thought we were building together. I walked away, my steps heavy, my mind a whirlwind of thoughts. I walked aimlessly, not knowing where I was going, not caring where I ended up. The city that had once been a symbol of our love, of our shared dreams and hopes, now seemed like a cruel reminder of my heartbreak.

Every street, every corner, every familiar sight was a painful reminder of what I had lost. The city, once vibrant and full of life, now seemed gray and lifeless. It was as if the city was mourning with me, sharing in my heartbreak.

As I walked, I realized that the city was not just a reminder of my heartbreak, but also a testament to my resilience. Yes, I was broken, yes, I was hurting, but I was also still standing. I was still here, still fighting, still hoping. And that gave me the strength to keep going, to keep moving forward, one step at a time. Because I knew, deep down, that this was not the end of my story, but merely the beginning of a new chapter. The days that followed were a blur, a surreal haze of disbelief and despair. I found myself wandering, my mind a whirlwind of thoughts and emotions. I was alone, truly alone for the first time in a long while. The silence was deafening, the emptiness, overwhelming. My heart ached with a pain so profound, it felt as if it would consume me.

Alicia, the woman I had loved with all my heart, had left me. She had taken with her not just her belongings, but my dreams, my hopes, my future. I felt as if I had been hollowed out, left a shell of the man I once was. I was heartbroken, lost in a sea of despair.

But amidst the pain and the heartbreak, a realization dawned upon me. It was a bitter truth, a harsh reality that I had been too blind to see. I had given Alicia the power to break me, to shatter my dreams. I had made her the center of my universe, the sun around which my world revolved. And when she left, my world collapsed.

But as the days turned into weeks, I began to see things in a different light. I realized that while Alicia had the power to break me, I also had the power to pick up the pieces and rebuild my life. I had the strength within me to rise from the ashes of my broken dreams and build a new future for myself.

I began to understand that my happiness, my future, my dreams - they were not tied to Alicia, or anyone else for that matter. They were mine to create, mine to nurture, mine to realize. I had the power to shape my destiny, to choose my path, to find my happiness.

And so, I made the conscious decision to turn the page, to start a new chapter in my life. I decided to rebuild myself from the ground up, to create a life that was not defined by my past, but by my present and my future.

I started by addressing the habits that had been detrimental to my well-being. I quit alcohol, a crutch I had leaned on heavily in the aftermath of my heartbreak. It was a difficult journey, fraught with temptation and setbacks, but I persevered. I replaced the empty bottles with healthier habits, like regular exercise and a balanced diet. I started taking care of my health, both physical and mental, realizing that it was the foundation upon which I could build my new life.

I reconnected with old friends, the ones I had neglected during my relationship with Alicia. I started going out more, experiencing the world outside the confines of my sorrow. I found solace in their company, in the shared laughter and camaraderie. I realized that I was not alone, that I had a support system that was there for me, ready to catch me when I fell.

I also rediscovered my love for painting, a passion I had abandoned when I was with Alicia. I picked up the brush again, letting the colors and strokes express what words could not. Each painting was a testament to my journey, a reflection of my emotions. It was therapeutic, a way for me to process my feelings and heal.

The journey was not easy. There were days when the pain was unbearable when I missed Alicia so much that it felt like a physical ache. But with each passing day, I found myself growing stronger, and more resilient. I realized that I was not just a man who had been heartbroken, I was a survivor. I was not defined by my past but by my ability to overcome it.

As I moved forward, I came to understand that Alicia was not the villain in my story. She was just a woman who was lost, just as I had been. She was trying to find her way, to navigate the complexities of love and relationships. I could not hate her for that. Instead, I found it in my heart to wish her happiness, to hope that she found what she was looking for.

In the end, I realized that my story was not about Alicia, it was about me. It was about my journey, my growth, my resilience. It was about finding the strength to pick up the pieces and rebuild, to create a life that was not defined by heartbreak, but by hope and perseverance. And in that realization, I found my peace. I found my redemption. I found myself.

I was left with more than just the remnants of a love that once was. I was left with a collage of memories, each one a snapshot of a moment in time, a moment of us. The laughter we shared, the dreams we dared to dream, the love we dared to love. Each memory was a reminder of what we had, a testament to a love that was as beautiful as it was heartbreaking.

But I was also left with something else, something deeper, something more profound. I was left with a deeper understanding of life and love. I realized that love was not just about joy and happiness, but also about pain and heartbreak. It was about the courage to love, to open your heart to someone, knowing that it could be broken. It was about the strength to love, to keep loving, even when it hurts.

I was left with a broken heart, a heart that was shattered into a million pieces. But I was also left with a stronger spirit. I realized that a broken heart was not a sign of weakness, but a sign of strength. It was a sign that I had truly loved, and that was something to be proud of.

I was left with the pain of loss, a pain that was raw and real. But I was also left with the hope of new beginnings. I realized that just as the sun sets, it also rises. Just as the seasons change, so do our lives. And just as a heart can break, it can also heal.

And in that, I found my peace. I found peace in the knowledge that I had loved and lost, but I had also grown and learned. I found peace in the knowledge that I had experienced the highest highs and the lowest lows, but I also found the strength to rise again. I found peace in the knowledge that I had been broken, but I had also been rebuilt.

And so, I moved forward, carrying with me the memories of our love, the lessons of our heartbreak, and the hope of new beginnings. I moved forward, not with a heavy heart, but with a stronger spirit. I moved forward, not with a sense of loss, but with a sense of hope. I moved forward, not as a man who was broken, but as a man who was rebuilt.

I realized that I was not just a man who had loved and lost. I was a man who had loved, lost and found himself. I was a man who had been broken but had also been rebuilt. I was a man who had experienced the pain of loss but had also experienced the hope of new beginnings. And in that, I found my peace. I found my redemption. I found myself. And in that newfound self, I found the courage to face each new day with hope and determination, ready to write the next chapter of my life. A chapter that was not defined by my past, but by my present and my future. A chapter that was not written by Alicia, but by me. And in that, I found my peace. I found my redemption. I found myself.

As the days turned into weeks, and weeks into months, I found myself slowly but surely rebuilding my life. I found solace in the simple things - the warmth of the morning sun on my face, the sound of rain against my window, and the smell of freshly brewed coffee. I found joy in my work, in my hobbies, and in the company of friends. I found strength in solitude, in resilience, in the ability to heal.

I began to travel, stepping out of the comfort of familiarity and venturing into the unknown. Each journey took me to places I had never been before - from the bustling streets of vibrant cities to the serene landscapes of the countryside. Each location was a new chapter in my life, filled with unique sights, sounds, and cultures that broadened my horizons and enriched my understanding of the world.

I met people from different walks of life, each person with a unique blend of experiences and perspectives. Conversations flowed like rivers, carrying stories of joy, sorrow, dreams, and struggles. These interactions opened my eyes to the diversity of human experience, teaching me empathy and understanding. They reminded me that everyone has their battles, their own stories, and their paths to healing.

Food, in its myriad forms, became a source of comfort and

discovery. I indulged in cuisines I had never tasted before, each dish a symphony of flavors that danced on my palate. From the spicy tang of street food to the refined flavors of gourmet meals, each culinary adventure was a celebration of culture and creativity. Food, in its unique way, told stories of places and people, of traditions and innovations.

Each new experience, each new encounter, was a step towards healing. They served as distractions, yes, but they were also reminders of the beauty and diversity of life. They helped me understand that life, despite its trials and tribulations, is a collection of experiences that shape us, mold us, and ultimately, heal us.

With each passing day, I felt myself becoming whole again. The fragments of my broken heart were slowly being pieced together, not to the way it was, but into something new, something stronger. The pain of the past was still there, but it was now a part of a larger picture - a picture of growth and an unyielding will to move forward. Through the journey of new experiences, I was not just healing; I was transforming. And in this transformation, I found the strength to embrace life once again, with all its ups and downs, with all its surprises and constants, with all its joys and sorrows.

One day, while walking in the park, I met a woman named Lily. She was kind, and compassionate, and had a smile that could light up a room. We started spending time together, sharing stories, laughing, and enjoying each other's company. I found myself drawn to Lily, not just because of her beauty, but because of her spirit, her zest for life, and her ability to find joy in the simplest things.

As I got to know Lily, I realized that I was falling in love again. It was a different kind of love, not the intense, passionate love I had for Alicia, but a gentle, comforting love. A love that healed, that soothed, that brought peace.

I was scared at first. I was scared of getting hurt, scared of losing again. But I also realized that love was a risk, a gamble. And I was willing to take that risk, for the chance to love and be loved again.

And so, I found myself not just surviving, but thriving. I found myself not just healing, but growing. I found myself not just living, but loving. And in that, I found peace. I found redemption.

My days began to fill with the light of Lily's presence. Her laughter was a melody that played in my heart, her words a balm to my soul. We spent countless hours together, exploring the city, sharing meals, and talking about everything under the sun. Lily's vibrant personality and zest for life breathed new life into my world.

One day, we decided to take a trip to the mountains. The serene beauty of the snow-capped peaks and the tranquil silence of the surroundings was a stark contrast to the bustling city life we were used to. It was here, amidst the grandeur of nature, that I realized the depth of my feelings for Lily.

I looked at her, her eyes reflecting the beauty of the setting sun, her hair dancing in the cool mountain breeze, and I knew that I had fallen in love with her. But this love was different from what I had felt for Alicia. It was quieter, softer, yet just as profound. It was a love born out of friendship and mutual respect, a love that healed instead of hurt.

I decided to confess my feelings to Lily. I was nervous, my heart pounding in my chest, but I knew I had to do it. I took a deep breath, looked into Lily's eyes, and told her how I felt. I told her about the love that had blossomed in my heart, a love that was as beautiful and serene as the mountains surrounding them.

Lily listened, her eyes wide with surprise. But then, she

smiled, a smile that warmed my heart. She confessed that she too had feelings for me, feelings that were just as profound. We embraced, our hearts beating in sync, our souls intertwined.

From that day forward, we became inseparable. We faced the world together, hand in hand, with our love a hope in our lives. I found myself smiling more, laughing more. I found myself looking forward to each new day, eager to see what it would bring.

My heart once shattered into a million pieces, was now whole again. But it was different. It was stronger, braver, more resilient. It was a heart that had known the depths of despair but had also known the heights of joy. It was a heart that had been broken but had also been mended.

I was no longer a man defined by his past, but a man shaped by his present, a man looking forward to his future. A future filled with love, hope, and endless possibilities. I found the courage to face each new day with hope and determination, ready to write the next chapter of my life. A chapter filled with love, joy, and a sense of fulfillment. A chapter that was not written by Alicia, but by me and Lily.

Just as I and Lily were settling into my newfound happiness, a letter arrived. It was an old, tattered envelope, addressed to Lily. The sender was someone named "James". Lily's face turned pale as she read the letter. It was from her childhood friend, James, who had disappeared years ago under mysterious circumstances.

James wrote that he had been living abroad, trying to forget his past, but he couldn't forget Lily. He confessed that he had always loved her, and he was now returning to claim his love.

This revelation shook my world. I felt a pang of jealousy and insecurity. But I also knew that I had to respect Lily's feelings. I decided to confront this situation with maturity and patience, ready to face whatever the future holds for me and Lily.

After reading James' letter, Lily was in a state of shock. She spent the next few days in deep thought, trying to understand her feelings. I gave her the space she needed, but the uncertainty was eating me up inside.

One evening, Lily asked me to take a walk with her. Under the starlit sky, she finally broke her silence. She told me about her past with James, their childhood friendship, and the bond they shared. But she also spoke about the love she had for me, the happiness she found in my presence and the future she envisioned with me.

She confessed that James' sudden reappearance had confused her. But after much thought, she realized that while she cared for James, it was I she truly loved. She didn't want to live in the past but wanted to move forward with me.

I felt a wave of relief wash over me. I held Lily close, promising to face any challenge that came our way together. From then on, our bond grew stronger. We faced many ups and downs, but our love for each other only deepened.

A few months later, I received an incredible job offer from a prestigious company located in a different city. It was the kind of opportunity that comes once in a lifetime. However, it meant moving away from the town where I and Lily had built our lives together.

Lily was happy for me, but the thought of leaving her job, her friends, and the life she loved filled her with apprehension. The decision to move wasn't easy for either of us. It was a test of our love and commitment to each other. We both spent countless nights discussing the pros and cons, trying to reach a decision that would be best for both of us. It was a stressful time, and the strain started to show in our relationship. There were disagreements, arguments, and tears.

But through it all, we remembered the love that we shared. We reassured each other that no matter what happened, we would face it together. This challenge, like the ones before, only served to strengthen our bond.

Lily decided to move with me. It was a difficult decision, but she believed in our love and was willing to make the sacrifice. The move was hard, and adjusting to the new city was even harder. But we were there for each other, supporting and encouraging one another.

This new challenge brought us closer together. It reminded us that love isn't just about the good times, but also about standing by each other during the tough times. It was another chapter in our love story, a chapter of growth, sacrifice, and enduring love.

As the days turned into weeks, and weeks into months, we began to find our rhythm in the new city. Lily found a job that she enjoyed, and I was doing well in my new role. We made new friends and explored new places, and slowly, the city that once felt so foreign started to feel like home.

But life, as it often does, had more challenges in store for us.

I was offered a promotion at work, which meant longer hours and more responsibilities. Lily was struggling with her challenges at work. The stress started to creep back into our lives, and once again, we found ourselves at a crossroads.

We knew we had to make changes to maintain our relationship and our sanity. We started by setting boundaries at work, making sure we had time for each other. We made it a point to have at least one meal together every day, where we would talk about anything but work. We also made sure to set aside time every week for a date night, just the two of us.

These changes didn't solve all our problems, but they helped. We were communicating more, spending more quality time together, and most importantly, we were happier. It was a reminder that love is not just about grand gestures and high emotions, but also about the small, everyday things that we do for each other.

As we settled into our new routine, we also started to explore the city more. We discovered quaint cafes, beautiful parks, and hidden gems that became our favorite spots. We also started to participate in local events and festivals, immersing ourselves in the culture of our new home.

One day, Lily came home with a surprise - she had adopted a puppy from a local shelter. The puppy, whom we named Bella, brought a new kind of joy and chaos into our lives.

We spent our days training her, playing with her, and simply enjoying the unconditional love she gave us.

Bella also helped us connect with our community. We met other dog owners in the park, joined a local pet club, and even volunteered at the shelter where we adopted Bella. These experiences not only enriched our lives but also deepened our bond.

However, life wasn't always perfect. We faced challenges, both individually and as a couple. There were times when we disagreed, when we hurt each other's feelings, and when we questioned our decisions. But each time, we chose to communicate, to understand, and to forgive. We chose love over conflict, understanding over judgment.

After a few years of living together, we realized that we were ready for the next step in our relationship. One beautiful evening, under the starlit sky at our favorite park, I proposed to Lily. It was a simple yet heartfelt proposal, and Lily, with tears in her eyes, said yes.

The wedding was a small, intimate affair with our closest

friends and family. We exchanged vows under the warm glow of the setting sun, promising to love and support each other through all of life's ups and downs. It was a beautiful day, filled with laughter, tears, and an overwhelming amount of love.

Married life brought its own set of challenges and joys. We learned to navigate our shared space, to compromise, and to solve disagreements respectfully and lovingly. We grew as individuals and as a couple, learning from each other and growing stronger together.

After the wedding, we went on our honeymoon, a trip to Europe that we had been dreaming of for years. We explored the romantic streets of Paris, the historic ruins in Rome, and the beautiful canals in Amsterdam. It was a magical time, a celebration of our love and the beginning of our new life together.

Upon our return, we decided to start a family. The news of Lily's pregnancy brought a new wave of excitement and anticipation. We spent the months preparing for the arrival of our baby, decorating the nursery, and imagining what our future as parents would look like.

When our daughter, Emma, was born, it was the most

beautiful moment of our lives. Holding her in our arms, we felt a love so profound and pure, that it was indescribable. Emma brought a new kind of love and joy into our lives. We watched her grow, marveling at every milestone, every smile, every step she took.

As parents, we faced new challenges and learned new lessons. We learned to balance our roles as parents, partners, and individuals. We learned patience, understanding, and the true meaning of unconditional love.

Through all the sleepless nights, the countless diaper changes, and the endless cycle of feedings, we found joy and fulfillment. We found strength in each other, and in the love, we had for our daughter.

As Emma grew, we found ourselves evolving as parents. We celebrated her first words, her first steps, and her first day of school. Each milestone was a testament to the love and care we had put into raising her.

We also made sure to keep our relationship strong. We continued our tradition of date nights, took family vacations, and made sure to spend quality time together. We faced challenges, of course, but we always found a way to overcome them together.

As Emma entered her teenage years, we faced a new set of challenges. There were disagreements and misunderstandings, but we navigated through them with patience and understanding. We learned to give her space when she needed it and to be there for her when she needed support.

Through all these years, our love for each other remained strong. We had grown from a young couple in love to a family, facing life's ups and downs together. Our journey was not always smooth, but it was filled with love, laughter, and countless memories.

And now, as we watch Emma grow into a beautiful, independent young woman, we can't help but feel a sense of pride and accomplishment.

As Emma transitioned into adulthood, we found ourselves transitioning too - from hands-on parents to advisors, from caretakers to confidants. We watched as Emma made her own decisions, learned from her mistakes, and carved out her path in life. It was a bittersweet time for us, filled with pride for the woman she was becoming, and nostalgia for the little girl she once was.

Emma chose to study environmental science in college, a

decision that reflected her passion for nature and her desire to make a difference in the world. We supported her decision and watched as she threw herself into her studies with enthusiasm and dedication.

During this time, Lily and I found ourselves with more time for each other. We rediscovered hobbies that we had put aside during our parenting years. Lily took up painting again, and I found joy in gardening. We also traveled more, exploring new places and cultures together.

Just as we were happy in our lives, an unexpected twist came in the form of Alicia, Lily's childhood friend. Alicia had been living abroad for many years and had recently moved back to our city. She reached out to Lily, and they reconnected as if no time had passed.

The name Alicia stirred a whirlpool of emotions within me. It was like opening a time capsule, the memories rushing back with an intensity that took my breath away. Alicia, the woman who had once been my world, was now sitting across from me, her eyes reflecting the same surprise that I felt.

I had spent years trying to forget her, to heal from the heartbreak she had left in her wake. And now, here she was, her presence turning my world upside down. The pain of the past mingled with the shock of the present, leaving me in a state of emotional turmoil.

But amidst the chaos, there was also a sense of closure.

Seeing Alicia again, I realized how much I had grown over the years. The heartbreak that had once shattered me now seemed like a distant memory, a stepping stone on my journey of self-discovery.

Alicia, too, was taken aback when she saw me. Her eyes widened in surprise, and for a moment, she was speechless. She had not expected our paths to cross again, especially not like this. But as the initial shock wore off, she regained her composure.

"I...I didn't know you were here, Jeremy," she stammered, her voice barely above a whisper. "It's been a long time."

"Yes, it has," I replied, my voice steady despite the whirlpool of emotions within me. "Life has a funny way of bringing people back together."

As we delved into the conversation, Alicia shared her experiences abroad, her voice tinged with a mix of nostalgia and regret. She spoke of her adventures, her achievements, and the life she had built. But amidst her stories, I could sense a hint of sadness, a longing for something that was lost.

Seeing Alicia again after all these years was like opening a book that had been closed for a long time. The chapters of our past were filled with memories of love and heartbreak.

But as we turned the pages, we realized that our story didn't end with heartbreak. It was just a part of our journey, a stepping stone to where we were today.

I had moved on, found love again, and built a life that I was proud of. While Alicia's sudden appearance stirred up old memories, it also provided me with an opportunity to finally put the past behind me.

We spent the afternoon reminiscing, acknowledging the mistakes we had made, and the lessons we had learned. It was a bittersweet reunion, filled with laughter, tears, and a mutual understanding that we had both moved on.

Alicia was no longer a painful memory, but a part of my past that had shaped me into the person I was today.

Life is filled with unexpected twists and turns, and Alicia's reappearance is one of them. But it was a reminder that no matter how painful the past might be, we have the strength to overcome it and the ability to find happiness again.

After they had gone, I asked Lily why didn't you mention Alicia was your friend?

Lily looked at me, her eyes filled with a mixture of surprise and regret. "I didn't think it was necessary to mention," she said, her voice barely above a whisper. "Alicia and I lost touch after she moved abroad. I had no idea she would be back."

I could see the sincerity in her eyes, but it did little to quell the storm of emotions brewing within me. I felt a pang of betrayal, mixed with a sense of confusion. Why hadn't Lily mentioned Alicia before? Was it an innocent oversight, or was there more to their friendship than she was letting on?

As these thoughts raced through my mind, I realized I needed to calm down and approach the situation rationally. I took a deep breath, reminding myself of the love and trust that Lily and I had built over the years.

"Lily," I began, my voice steady despite the turmoil within. "Alicia and I have a history. She was my first love, and she broke my heart when she left. Seeing her again after all these years has brought back a lot of old feelings."

Lily listened quietly, her eyes reflecting the pain that my words must have caused her. When I finished, she reached out and took my hand, giving it a reassuring squeeze. "I'm sorry," she said. "I had no idea. But you need to know that whatever happened in the past, it doesn't change the way I feel about you."

Her sincere words were a balm to my unsettled heart. We spent the rest of the evening talking, opening up about our pasts, our fears, and our hopes for the future. It was a difficult conversation, but it was also a necessary one. It helped us understand each other better and brought us closer than ever. The encounter with Alicia served as a reminder of our past, but it also reinforced the strength of our love in the present. We realized that while our past had shaped us, it was our present and future together that truly mattered.

Alicia's presence in our lives turned out to be a blessing in disguise. She brought back old memories, but she also helped us create new ones. Alicia, Lily, and I found a unique friendship that was built on understanding, respect, and shared history.

As the days turned into weeks, and weeks into months, Alicia became a part of our lives. We shared meals, went on trips, and celebrated festivals together. Alicia, who had once been a source of heartbreak, was now a part of our family.

Life is indeed filled with unexpected twists and turns, but it's these twists that make our journey interesting. They test our strengths, challenge our beliefs and ultimately shape us into the people we become.

One sunny afternoon, our doorbell rang. As I opened the door, I was greeted by a familiar face, Alicia, her radiant smile as warm as ever. But she wasn't alone. Standing beside her was a handsome man who had a striking resemblance to her, and two young adults, a boy and a girl, who were their children.

Alicia introduced the man as her husband, Alex. He had a kind demeanor and a gentle smile. Their son, Ethan, had his mother's eyes and his father's charismatic personality. He was in his early twenties, just starting his journey into adulthood. Their daughter, Olivia, was a bit older than our Emma. She had a quiet elegance about her and a maturity that was well beyond her years.

As they stepped into our home, there was a moment of hesitation, a brief interlude before our worlds collided. But as soon as Lily and Emma joined us, the room was filled with warmth and laughter. The initial awkwardness evaporated, replaced by animated conversations and shared stories.

We spent the afternoon getting to know each other. Alex shared tales of their adventures abroad, and Ethan spoke about his college experiences, and Olivia, who was preparing to start university, listened with rapt attention to Emma's high school stories.

As the days passed, Alicia and her family became a regular part of our lives. Our homes were always open to each other, and our families shared meals, holidays, and important life events. The children, despite the age difference, formed a close bond, their laughter and chatter a constant source of joy.

Alicia and Alex, with their worldly experiences and diverse backgrounds, brought a new perspective to our lives. We learned from them, and they from us. This exchange of ideas and experiences enriched our lives in ways we hadn't anticipated.

One day, Alicia proposed an idea - a joint vacation for both our families. The idea was met with enthusiastic agreement, and we found ourselves planning a trip to the mountains. The vacation was a memorable one, filled with adventure, bonding, and the creation of beautiful memories.

Life, with all its twists and turns, had brought us to a place of contentment and happiness. Our story, which had started with heartbreak, had evolved into a tale of love, friendship, and family. Alicia, who had once been a source of pain, was now a part of our happiness.

As we continued on our journey, we realized that our love story was not just about us. It was about all the people who were a part of our lives - our friends, our families, and everyone who had touched our lives in some way.

Our lives continued to evolve with Alicia and her family becoming an integral part of it. The children, now young adults, were making their way in the world. Emma followed in her mother's footsteps and pursued a career in environmental science. Olivia, inspired by her parents, chose to study international relations, while Ethan was making a name for himself in the tech industry.

We watched with pride as they grew into responsible and compassionate individuals, their successes a testament to their hard work and dedication. They were not just our children anymore, but also our friends, their lives intertwining with ours in shared experiences and mutual respect.

Alicia and Alex, too, had become more than just friends. They were our family, their presence in our lives a constant source of joy and comfort. We shared our hopes and fears, our triumphs and failures, and in doing so, we learned from each other and grew together.

Heartbreak and depression are incredibly challenging to navigate. They can make the world seem bleak and devoid of joy. However, it's important to remember that these feelings are temporary and that healing is possible.

1. **Acknowledge Your Feelings**: It's okay to grieve the loss of a relationship. Allow yourself to feel the pain, but don't let it define you. Your feelings are valid, and acknowledging them is the first step towards healing.

2. **Reach Out**: Don't isolate yourself. Reach out to trusted friends and family members. Share your feelings with them. You'd be surprised how much talking about your feelings can help.

3. **Self-Care**: Engage in activities that you love. This could be reading, painting, hiking, or anything that brings you joy and peace. Taking care of your physical health can also impact your emotional well-being.

4. **Seek Professional Help**: If your feelings of sadness become overwhelming, don't hesitate to seek professional help. Therapists and counselors are trained to help you navigate through your feelings and can provide you with tools and strategies to cope.

5. **Give Yourself Time**: Healing takes time. Don't rush yourself or let others rush you. It's okay to move at your own pace.

6. **Forgive and Let Go**: Holding onto anger and resentment can hinder your healing process. Try to forgive, not for the other person, but for yourself.

7. **Embrace Change**: Accept that change is a part of life. Try to embrace it instead of resisting it. Remember, every end is a new beginning.

8. **Give Life Another Chance**: Despite the pain, try to stay open to the possibility of love and happiness. Believe in the potential of a brighter future. Giving life another chance means giving yourself another chance at happiness.

9. **Rediscover Yourself:** Use this time to reconnect with yourself. Explore your interests, develop new hobbies, and spend time doing things that you love. This can help you regain your sense of self-worth and

confidence.

10. **Practice Mindfulness**: Mindfulness involves focusing on the present moment without judgment. It can help you manage your emotions and improve your mental well-being. There are various ways to practice mindfulness, such as meditation, yoga, or simply taking a few minutes each day to focus on your breath.

11. **Cultivate Positivity**: Try to maintain a positive outlook even in tough times. Surround yourself with positive people, engage in activities that make you happy, and practice gratitude. Cultivating positivity can help you cope with negative emotions and lead to a happier, healthier mindset.

12. **Set Personal Goals**: Setting personal goals can give you something to look forward to and can help you feel more in control of your life. These goals can be related to your career, personal growth, or hobbies.

13. **Embrace Life**: Remember that life is full of ups and downs. It's okay to have bad days. What's important is that you don't lose hope and continue to move forward. Embrace life with all its challenges and joys.

14. **Remember, You Are Not Alone**: It's easy to feel isolated when you're going through a tough time, but remember, you are not alone. Some people care about you and want to help. Don't hesitate to reach out to them.

15. **Believe in Yourself**: Believe in your strength and resilience. You have overcome challenges before, and you can do it again. Believe in your ability to heal, to grow, and to find happiness again.

Remember, healing is a journey, and it's okay to take it one day at a time. Be patient with yourself, and don't rush the process. And most importantly, remember that it's okay to give life another chance. You are worthy of love, happiness, and all the good things that life has to offer. Don't let your past define your future. You have the power to write your own story, and it can be as beautiful as you choose to make it.

9 798224 049332